This igloo book belongs to:

karahi

This edition published in 2012
by Igloo Books Ltd
Cottage Farm,
Sywell, NN6 0BJ
www.igloo-books.com

REX001 0612

2 4 6 8 10 9 7 5 3

ISBN: 978-0-85780-431-0

Printed and manufactured in China

Puppy's Big Rescue!

igloo

Little Puppy was very proud of his dad, who had just won a blue ribbon for being a champion sheep dog. "One day, I'm going to win a blue ribbon just like you," said Little Puppy.

"To be a top sheep dog," said his dad, "you need to be able to move quickly and listen very carefully to what you are told."

But Little Puppy was not listening. Nearby, he could see his friends running towards a big oak tree.

At the oak tree, Little Puppy looked up to see a beehive.
"I'm going to see if there is any honey inside," he said.
"Watch out for the bees, Little Puppy!" called out his friends.

But Little Puppy was not listening.
As he put his paw into the beehive,
a loud buzzing sound filled the air.

BUZZZZZZZZZZZZZZ!

Little Puppy ran away as fast as he could, then... SPLASH!
He landed right in the middle of a muddy pond.

"BRRR! The water is f-f-freezing,"
said Little Puppy, shivering.
"I had better shake myself dry,
before I catch a cold."
"Stop, Little Puppy!"
shouted his friends. "Or you will
get us all wet!"

But Little Puppy was not listening. As he shook and shook and shook, he covered his friends in water.

"Look at Ram," laughed Little Puppy, "he's soaking wet!"
"I wouldn't be wet if you had listened," bleated Ram.

Ram chased Little Puppy out of the pond, down the lane, through the gate and across the farmyard straight into a...

...slimy, stinky pile of squelchy muck!

"Are you alright?" asked Little Puppy's friends.
"No, I'm not," he whimpered. "I'm fed up, tired and very smelly!"

That evening, Little Puppy settled
down for a sleep with his dad.
"I'll never be a good sheep dog," he sighed,
unhappily. "I always seem to end up in trouble."

"You just need to listen, Little Puppy," said his dad, softly. "Then you will know what to do next." "All I can hear right now are snoring animals," yawned Little Puppy, as he drifted off to sleep.

In the middle of the night, Little Puppy suddenly woke up.
"Baa! Baa!"
"That sounds like Ram," thought Little Puppy. He got up
and crept quickly out of the barn, just in time to
see a dark shape slinking towards the sheep — a fox!

Little Puppy bounded towards the fox, barking as loudly as
he could. "Get away from my sheep," he barked as the frightened
fox ran back across the hill.

"I'm so glad you heard my bleats for help, Little Puppy," said Ram, the next day. The farm animals all agreed that Little Puppy deserved a very special reward for being so brave.

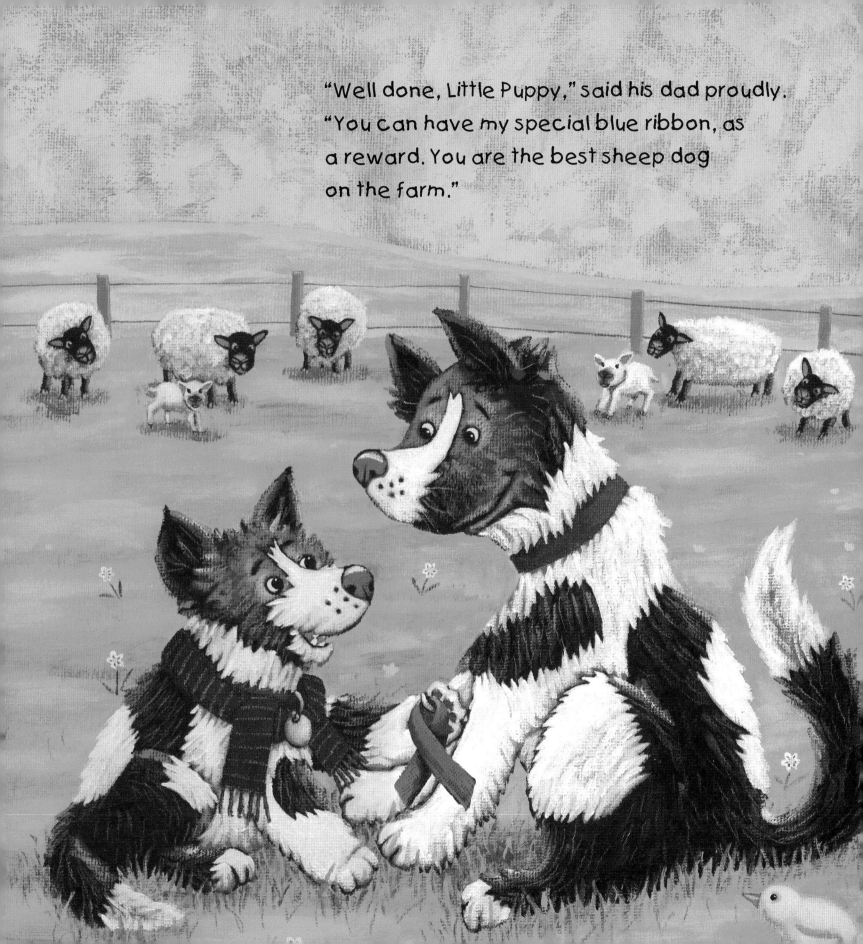

"Well done, Little Puppy," said his dad proudly.
"You can have my special blue ribbon, as
a reward. You are the best sheep dog
on the farm."

"Goodbye, see you soon!"